PUFFIN BOOKS

THE OTTERS' TALE

For more than ten years Gavin Maxwell lived with his otter companions in a house called Camusfeàrna, at the edge of the sea and in a wild and lonely part of the Scottish Highlands. First there was Mijbil, then Edal, and later Teko.

It all started with Mijbil, and from his first sight of the bedraggled bundle of spiky fur, and the first crash of breaking china, Gavin Maxwell knew his life would be changed for ever. After a few days the otter had accepted him completely, and from then on they began to get to know each other. They shared the same bed, the same bath, and hours of play together. They moved from Southern Iraq, via London, to the freedom of Camusfeàrna. There Mij became a real part of the surroundings – living in the house, exploring, and taking a mischievous interest in everything, enjoying the sea, and providing endless hours of fascination for the author. But, sadly, before Gavin Maxwell could spend another summer with Mij their life together was over.

Gavin Maxwell spent a year away from Camusfeàrna and another year looking for an otter to fill the empty place left by Mij. When he had almost given up hope he came across Edal, six months old and almost certainly destined for life in a zoo. Originally from West Africa, Edal soon settled down in Camusfeàrna and proved to be a delightful companion. Another otter, Teko, joined the company the following summer, and although at first he wasn't accepted by Edal, he, too, soon became part of Camusfeàrna, and the otters' tale.

Illustrated with photographs taken by the author.

GAVIN MAXWELL

The Otters' Tale

PUFFIN BOOKS

PUFFIN BOOKS

Published by the Penguin Group
27 Wrights Lane, London w8 5tz, England
Viking Penguin Inc., 40 West 23rd Street, New York, New York 10010, USA
Penguin Books Australia Ltd, Ringwood, Victoria, Australia
Penguin Books Canada Ltd, 2801 John Street, Markham, Ontario, Canada l3r 1b4
Penguin Books (NZ) Ltd, 182–190 Wairau Road, Auckland 10, New Zealand

Penguin Books Ltd, Registered Offices: Harmondsworth, Middlesex, England

First published by Longmans 1962
Published in Puffin Books 1977
7 9 10 8 6

Made and printed in Great Britain by
Richard Clay Ltd, Bungay, Suffolk
Set in Linotype Georgian

'*To all, but more particularly children, who also seek understanding between humans and other animals.*'

Contents

Author's Foreword

SINCE the publication of *Ring of Bright Water* in September 1960 I have received a great number of letters asking for a new and shortened edition suitable for children, an edition that would tell the story of the otters only and omit the more difficult words in the text of the original. This I have done, and I hope that some of the thousands of adults who have written to me may also find some pleasure in the introduction of the new otter, Teko.

This foreword should contain, too, a word of warning. It is now the ambition of many of my correspondents to keep an otter themselves, and I feel that I should stress again that for the vast majority of people otters are not a practical proposition. They are wild animals, and very active ones at that; to keep them contented and healthy in a domesticated state is a full-time and a very expensive job, and if they are not contented they behave as most unhappy animals and humans do and become ill-tempered. Just as a happy otter is a more entertaining, affectionate and intelligent creature than most dogs, so an unhappy and discontented otter can be more surly – and in the long run far more dangerous – than a dog. As travel books are often written for those who would like to travel but for one reason or another are not able to do so, so this book is for those who would like to keep otters but cannot.

All photographs were taken by me. I am indebted to the *Daily Mail* for permission to reprint certain parts of Chapters 5 and 6, which first appeared in that newspaper.

Publisher's note:

The sequel to *Ring of Bright Water* is called *The Rocks Remain*, and carries the story up until September 1966, when Camusfeàrna, the house where Gavin Maxwell lived with the otters, was burned to the ground. Gavin Maxwell died in 1969.

I

Mijbil–Iraq to London

I SIT in a pitch-pine panelled kitchen–living room, with an otter asleep upon its back among the cushions on the sofa, forepaws in the air, and with the expression of tightly shut concentration that very small babies wear in sleep. Beyond the door is the sea, whose waves break on the beach no more than a stone's throw distant, and encircling, mist-hung mountains. A little group of Greylag geese sweep past the window and alight upon the small carpet of green turf; but for the soft, contented murmur of their voices and the sounds of the sea and the waterfall there is utter silence. This place has been my home now for ten years and more. It is also the home of two otters, Edal and Teko, and once it was the home of Mijbil, who first taught me what wonderful creatures otters are. The house is called Camusfeàrna, and it stands right at the edge of the sea in a wild and lonely part of the Scottish Highlands.

Mijbil's story begins a long way from Camus-feàrna, for he came from the great marshes of Southern Iraq, where the Tigris joins the Euphrates. A few years ago I travelled with Wilfred Thesiger, the explorer, to spend two months or so among the little-known Marsh Arabs, who live there. By then it had crossed my mind that I should like to keep an otter, and that Camusfeàrna, ringed by water a stone's throw from its door, would be the right place for this experiment. I had mentioned this to Wilfred soon after the start of our journey, and he had replied that I had better get one in the Tigris marshes before I came home, for there they were as common as mosquitoes, and were often tamed by the Arabs.

We spent the better part of those two months squatting cross-legged in the bottom of a war canoe, travelling between the scattered reed-built villages; and at the end of our journey I did acquire an otter cub.

Wilfred Thesiger and I were both going to Basra, the nearest big town, to collect and answer our letters from home before setting off together again, but when we got there we found that Wilfred's mail had arrived but that mine had not, so I arranged to join Thesiger in a week's time, and he left without me.

Two days before the date of our rendezvous I returned to the Consulate–General, where I was living, late in the afternoon, having been out for several hours, to find my mail had arrived. I carried it to my bedroom to read, and there squatting on the floor were two Marsh Arabs; beside them lay a sack that squirmed from time to time.

They handed me a note from Wilfred. 'Here is your otter, a male and weaned. I feel you may want to take it to London – it would be a handful in the canoe.'

With the opening of that sack began a phase of my life that has not yet ended, and may, for all I know, not end before I do, because I can't any longer imagine being without an otter in the household.

The creature that emerged, from this sack on to the spacious tiled floor of the Consulate bedroom, did not at that moment look like anything so much as a very small dragon. From the head to the tip of the tail it was coated with pointed scales of mud armour, between whose tips you could see a soft velvet fur like that of a chocolate-brown mole. He shook himself, and I half expected a cloud of dust, but the mud stayed where it was, and in fact it was not for another month that I managed to remove the last of it and see him, so to speak, in his true colours.

For the first twenty-four hours Mijbil was neither friendly nor unfriendly; he was simply aloof and indifferent, choosing to sleep on the floor as far from my bed as possible, and to accept food and water as though they were things that had appeared

before him without human help. He ate small red-
dish fish from the Tigris, holding them upright between his forepaws, tail end uppermost, and eating
them like a stick of Edinburgh rock, always with
five crunches on the left-hand side of the jaw
alternating with five crunches on the right.

The otter and I enjoyed the Consul-General's
long-suffering hospitality for a fortnight. The second night Mijbil came to my bed in the small hours
and remained asleep in the crook of my knees until
the servant brought tea in the morning and during
that day he began to lose his sulks and take a keen,
much too keen, interest in his surroundings. I made
a collar, or rather a body-belt, for him, and took
him on a lead to the bathroom, where for half an
hour he went wild with joy in the water, plunging
and rolling in it, shooting up and down the length
of the bath underwater, and making enough slosh
and splash for a hippo. This, I was to learn, is what
otters do; every drop of water must be spread about
the place; a bowl must at once be upset, or, if it
will not overturn, be sat in and sploshed in until it
overflows. Water must be kept on the move and
made to do things.

It was only two days later that he escaped from
my bedroom as I entered it, and I turned to see his
tail disappearing round the bend of the corridor
that led to the bathroom. By the time I had caught
up with him he was up on the end of the bath and

fumbling at the chromium taps with his paws. I watched, amazed; in less than a minute he had turned the tap far enough to produce a dribble of water, and, after a moment or two, the full flow. (He had, in fact, been lucky to turn the tap right way; later he would as often as not try with great violence to screw it up still tighter, chittering with annoyance and disappointment at his failure.)

After a few days he would follow me without a lead and come to me when I called his name. By the end of a week he had accepted me completely and then he began to play. Very few species of animal play much after they are grown up; but otters are one of the exceptions to this rule; right through their lives they spend much of their time in play that does not even need a partner. In the wild state they will play alone for hours with some floating object in the water, pulling it down to let it bob up again, or throwing it with a jerk of the head so that it lands with a splash and becomes something to be chased. No doubt in their holts they lie on their backs and play too, as my otters have, with small objects that they can roll between their paws and pass from palm to palm, for at Camusfeàrna all the sea holts contain small shells and round stones that can only have been carried in for toys.

Mij would spend hours shuffling a rubber ball round the room like a four-footed soccer player using all four feet to dribble the ball, and he could also throw it, with a powerful flick of the neck, to a surprising height and distance. These games he would play either by himself or with me, but the really steady play of an otter, the time-filling play born of a sense of well-being and a full stomach, seems to me to be when the otter lies on its back and juggles with small objects between its paws. Marbles became Mij's favourite toys for this pastime and he would lie on his back rolling two or more of them up and down his wide, flat belly without ever dropping one to the floor, or, with forepaws upstretched, rolling them between his palms for minutes on end.

Even during that first fortnight in Basra I learnt a lot of Mij's language. The sounds are widely different in range. The simplest is the call note, which has been much the same in all the otters I have come across; it is a short, anxious, mixture between a whistle and a chirp, and it can be heard for a long way. There is also a query, used at closer quarters; Mij would enter a room, for instance, and ask whether there was anyone in it by the word 'Ha!', in a loud, harsh whisper. But it was the chirp, high or low, from the single note to a continuous flow of chitter, that was Mij's main means of talk.

An otter's jaws are, of course, very strong and those jaws have teeth meant to crunch into pulp fish heads that seem as hard as stone. Like a puppy that nibbles and gnaws one's hands because he has so few other outlets for his feelings, otters seem to find the use of their mouths the most natural thing; knowing as I do their enormous crushing power I can see how hard my otters have tried to be gentle in play, but perhaps they think a human skin is as thick as an otter's. Mij used to look hurt and surprised when scolded for what must have seemed to him real gentleness, and though after a time he learned to be as soft-mouthed as a sucking dove with me, he remained all his life somewhat over-excitably good-humoured and hail-fellow-well-bit with strangers.

The days passed peacefully at Basra, but I dreaded the prospect of transporting Mij to England, and to Camusfeàrna. The Air Line insisted that Mij should be packed into a box of not more than eighteen inches square, and that this box must be personal luggage, to be carried on the floor at my feet.

The box was delivered on the afternoon before my departure on a 9.15 p.m. flight. It was zinc-lined and it seemed to me as nearly ideal as could be.

Dinner was at eight, and I thought that it would be as well to put Mij into the box an hour before we left, so that he would become accustomed to it before the jolting of the journey began to upset him. I got him into it, not without difficulty, and he seemed peaceful when I left him in the dark for a hurried meal.

But when I came back, with only barely time for the Consulate car to reach the airport for the flight, I saw an awful sight. There was complete silence from inside the box, but from its airholes and the chinks around the hinged lid, blood had trickled and dried on the white wood. I whipped off the padlock and tore open the lid, and Mij, exhausted and blood-spattered, whimpered and tried to climb up my leg. He had torn the zinc lining to shreds, scratching his mouth, his nose and his paws, and had left it jutting in spiky ribbons all around the walls and the floor of the box. When I had removed the last of it, so that there were no cutting edges left, it was just ten minutes until the time of the flight, and the airport was five miles distant. It was hard to bring myself to put the miserable Mij back into that box, that now seemed to him a torture chamber, but I forced myself to do it, slamming the lid down on my fingers as I closed it before he could make his escape. Then began a journey the like of which I hope I shall never know again.

I sat in the back of the car with the box beside me as the Arab driver tore through the streets of Basra like a bullet. Donkeys reared, bicycles swerved wildly, out in the suburbs goats stampeded and poultry found unguessed powers of flight. Mij cried unceasingly in the box, and both of us were hurled to and fro and up and down like drinks in a cocktail shaker. Exactly as we drew to a screeching stop before the airport entrance I heard a splintering sound from the box beside me, and saw Mij's nose force up the lid. He had summoned all the strength in his small body and torn one of the hinges clean out of the wood.

The aircraft was waiting to take off; as I was rushed through the customs by infuriated officials I was trying all the time to hold down the lid of the box with one hand, and with the other to force back the screws into the splintered wood.

It was perhaps my only stroke of fortune that the seat booked for me was at the extreme front of the aircraft, so that I had a bulkhead before me instead of another seat.

The port engines roared and then the starboard, and the aircraft trembled and teetered against the tug of her propellers, and then we were taxiing out to take off. Ten minutes later we were flying westwards over the great marshes that had been Mij's home, and peering downward into the dark I could see the glint of their waters beneath the moon.

I had brought a briefcase full of old newspapers, and a parcel of fish, and with these scant resources I prepared myself to withstand a siege.

I unlocked the padlock and opened the lid, and Mij was out like a flash. He dodged my fumbling hands with an eel-like wriggle and disappeared at high speed down the fuselage of the aircraft. As I tried to get into the gangway I could follow his progress among the passengers by a wave of disturbance among them not unlike that caused by the passage of a stoat through a hen run. There were squawks and shrieks and a flapping of travelling-coats, and halfway down the fuselage a woman stood up on her seat screaming out, 'A rat! A rat!'

I ran down the gangway and, catching sight of Mij's tail disappearing beneath the legs of a portly white-turbaned Indian, I tried a flying tackle, landing flat on my face. I missed Mij's tail, but found myself grasping the sandalled foot of the Indian's female companion; furthermore my face was inexplicably covered in curry. I staggered up babbling apology, and the Indian gave me a long silent stare, so blank that I could deduce from it no meaning whatsoever. I was, however, glad to see that something, possibly the curry, had won over the bulk of my fellow-passengers, and that they were regarding me now as a harmless clown rather than as a dangerous lunatic. The air hostess stepped into the breach.

'Perhaps,' she said with the most charming smile, 'it would be better if you resumed your seat, and I will find the animal and bring it to you.' I explained that Mij, being lost and frightened, might bite a stranger, but she did not think so. I returned to my seat.

I heard the ripple of flight and pursuit passing up and down the body of the aircraft behind me, but I could see little. I was craning my neck back over the seat trying to follow the hunt when suddenly I heard from my feet a distressed chitter of recognition and welcome, and Mij bounded on to my knee and began to nuzzle my face and neck. In all the strange world of the aircraft I was the only familiar thing to be found, and in that first return to me was sown the seed of the absolute trust that he gave me for the rest of his life.

Otters are extremely bad at doing nothing. That is to say that they cannot, as a dog does, lie still and awake; they are either asleep or entirely absorbed in play. If there is no toy, or if they are bored, they will set about laying the land waste. There is, I am convinced, something positively provoking to an otter about order and tidiness in any form, and the greater the untidiness that they can make the more contented they feel. A room does not seem right to them until they have turned everything upside down; cushions must be thrown to the floor from sofas and armchairs, books pulled out of bookcases, wastepaper baskets overturned and the rubbish spread as widely as possible, drawers opened and contents shovelled out and scattered. An otter must find out everything and have a hand in everything; but most of all he must know what lies inside any man-made container or beyond any man-made obstruction.

We had been flying for perhaps five hours when one of these moods descended upon Mijbil. It opened fairly harmlessly, with an attack upon the newspapers spread carefully round my feet, and in a minute or two the place looked like a street upon which royalty has been given a ticker-tape welcome. Then he turned his attentions to the box, where his sleeping compartment was filled with fine wood-shavings. First he put his head and shoulders in and began to throw these out backwards at enormous speed; then he got in bodily and lay on his back, using all four feet in a pedalling motion to hoist out the rest. I was doing my best to cope with the litter, but it was like a ship's pumps working against a leak too great for them, and I was hopelessly behind in the race when he turned his attention to my neighbour's canvas Trans-World travel bag on the floor beside him. The zipper gave him pause for no more than seconds; by chance, probably, he yanked it back and was in head first throwing out magazines, handkerchiefs, bottles of pills and tins of ear-plugs. By the grace of God my neighbour was asleep; I managed, unobserved, to haul Mij out by the tail and cram the things back somehow. I hoped that she might leave the aircraft at Cairo, before the outrage was discovered, and to my infinite relief she did so.

My troubles really began at Paris, a long time later. Mij had slept from time to time, but I had not closed an eye, and it was by now more than thirty-six hours since I had even dozed. I had to change airports, and, since I knew that Mij could slip his body strap with the least struggle, there was nothing else to do but put him back in his box. In its present form, however, the box was useless, for one hinge was dangling unattached from the lid.

I explained my predicament to the air hostess. She went forward to the crew's quarters, and returned after a few minutes saying that one of the crew would come and nail down the box and rope it for me. She warned me at the same time that Air France's rules differed from those of Trans-World, and that from Paris onward the box would have to travel freight and not in the passenger portion of the aircraft.

Mij was sleeping on his back inside my jacket, and I had to steel myself to betray his trust, to force him back into that hateful prison and listen to his pathetic cries as he was nailed in what now seemed to me like a coffin.

It was the small hours of the morning when we reached London Airport at last. I had cabled London and there was a hired car to meet me.

Mij, who had slept ever since the box was nailed up, was wide awake once more by the time we reached my flat; and when I had the driver paid off and the door closed behind me I prised open the lid of the box, and Mij clambered out into my arms to greet me with a frenzy of affection that I felt I had hardly deserved

2

Life with Mijbil

OTTERS that have been reared by human beings
demand human company, much affection, and
constant play; without these things they quickly
become unhappy, and that makes them tiresome.

The spacious tile-floored bedroom of the Consulate–General at Basra, with its minimum of
furniture or bric-à-brac, had done little to prepare
me for the problems that my crowded studio
would present. Exhausted as he was that first
night, Mij had not been out of his box for five
minutes before he set out to explore his new
quarters. I had gone to the kitchen to find fish for
him, which I had arranged with my charlady to
leave, but I had hardly got there before I heard the
first crash of breaking china in the room behind
me. The fish and the bath solved the problem for
a while, for when he had eaten he went wild with
joy in the water and romped for a full half hour,
but it was clear that the flat would require a lot
of alteration if it was to remain a home for both
of us. Meanwhile sleep seemed long overdue, and
I saw only one solution; I laid a sleeping-bag on

the sofa, and anchored Mij to the sofa-leg by his lead.

Mij seemed to watch me closely as I composed myself on my back with a cushion under my head; then, with an air of knowing exactly what to do, he clambered up beside me and worked his body down into the sleeping-bag until he lay flat on his back inside it with his head on the cushion beside mine and his fore-paws in the air. In this position he heaved an enormous sigh and was instantly asleep.

Mij and I stayed in London for nearly a month, while, as my landlord put it, the studio came to look like a cross between a monkey-house and a furniture dump. A wire gate was fitted to the gallery stairs, so that he could sometimes be shut out of the studio itself; the upstairs telephone was enclosed in a box (whose fastening he early learned to undo); my dressing-table was cut off from him by a wire flap hinged from the ceiling, and the electric light wires were enclosed in tunnels of hardboard that made the place look like a power-house.

When he was loose in the studio, he would play for hours at a time with his favourite toys, ping-pong balls, marbles, indiarubber fruit and a terra-pin shell that I had brought back from his native marshes. The smaller among these objects he could throw right across the room with a flick of his head, and with a ping-pong ball he invented a game of his own which would keep him happy for up to half an hour at a time. An expanding suitcase that I had taken to Iraq had become damaged on the journey home, so that the lid, when closed, remained at a slope from one end to the other. Mij discovered that if he put the ball on the high end it would run down the length of the suitcase unaided. He would dash round to the other end to ambush its arrival, hide from it, crouching, to spring up and take it by surprise as it reached the drop to the floor, grab it and trot off with it to the high end once more.

These games were enough for perhaps half of all the time he spent indoors and awake, but several times a day he needed a long romp with a human playmate. Tunnelling under the carpet and making believe that in doing so he became invisible, he would shoot out with a squeak of triumph if a foot passed within range; or he would dive inside the loose cover of the sofa and play tigers from behind it; or he would simply lay siege to one's person as a puppy does, bouncing around one in a frenzy of excited chirps and squeaks and launching a series of tip-and-run raids.

I soon found a way to distract his attention if he became too excitable. I would take the terrapin shell, wrap it in a towel, and knot the loose ends tightly across. He came to know these preparations, and would wait absolutely motionless until I handed him the bundle; then he would straddle it with his fore-arms, sink his teeth in the knots, and begin to hump and shuffle round the room. No matter how difficult the knots he would have them all undone in five or ten minutes, and then bring the towel and the terrapin shell to be tied up again. He brought the towel first, dragging it, and then made a second trip for the terrapin, shuffling it in front of him down the room like a football.

At night he slept in my bed, still, at this time, on his back with his head on the pillow, and in the morning he shared my bath. He would plunge ahead of me into water still too hot for me to enter, and while I shaved he would swim round me playing with the soapsuds or with celluloid and rubber ducks and ships.

Outside the house I took him for walks on a lead, just as if he had been a dog.

I was too timid of the result to allow him to meet any dog so to speak nose to nose, and I would pick him up if we met unattended dogs in the street, but for his part he seemed largely indifferent to them. The only time that I felt he knew that he had something in common with dogs was one morning when, setting out for his walk, he refused to be parted from a new toy, a large rubber ball painted in gaudy segments. This ball was too big for his mouth, so that he could only carry it sticking out from one side of his jaws like a gigantic gumboil, and thus burdened he set off briskly up the street, tugging at his lead. Rounding the first street corner we came face to face with a very fat spaniel, alone and carrying in his mouth a bundle of newspapers. The loads of the otter and the dog made it difficult for either of them to turn its head far as they came abreast, but their eyes rolled sideways with what appeared to me a wild surmise, and when they were a few paces past each other both suddenly stopped dead for a moment, as though each had suddenly realized something new.

It was not lack of curiosity, so much as lack of time and opportunity, that made me delay for nearly three weeks before making any real effort to find out Mij's race.

It is not, I suppose, in any way strange that most Londoners should not recognize an otter. Otters belong to a small group of animals called Mustellines, shared by the badger, mongoose, weasel, stoat, polecat, marten, mink and others. In the London streets, I faced continual questions that mentioned all the Mustellines but the otter; wilder, more random fire hit on practically everything from 'a baby seal' to a squirrel. The seal idea had deep root, and was perhaps the commonest of them all, though far from being the most odd. 'Is that a walrus, mister?' reduced me to giggles outside Harrods, and 'a hippo' made my day outside Cruft's Dog Show. A beaver, a bear cub, a newt, a leopard – one, apparently, that had changed his spots – even a 'brontosaur'; Mij was anything but an otter.

At last I telephoned to the Natural History department of the British Museum, in Cromwell Road, and the same afternoon Mr Robert Hayman arrived at my flat to examine two skins I had bought in Iraq and the living Mijbil, and in due course, Mij's new race was proclaimed. Hayman summoned me to the Museum to see the cabinets of otter skins from all over Asia, where the larger of mine lay, unlabelled and quite different from any other, in a drawer by itself, but beside its nearest relatives. These were of a variety of hues from pale sandy to medium brown, but none had been recorded west of Sind, in India, and none resembled mine in colour.

There are very few people who stumble upon a sizeable mammal previously unknown to science; in the nursery world of picture-books of birds and beasts the few who had given their own names to species – Steller's Eider and Sea Eagle, Sharpe's Crow, Humboldt's Woolly Monkey, Meinerzthagen's Forest Hog, Ross's Snow Goose, Grant's Gazelle, Père David's Deer – had been something like gods to me; they seemed like creators. Now, when Hayman suggested that the new otter should bear my name, something small and shrill from the nursery days was shouting inside me that I could become one of these gods and wear the halo of a creator. 'Can I have it for my own?' we used to ask when we were small. 'For my *very* own?' Here, surely, was an animal of my very own, to bear my name; every animal that looked like it would always bear my name for ever and ever.

So Mij and all his race became *Lutrogale perspicillata maxwelli*, and though he is now no more, and there is no real proof that there is another of his kind living in the world, I had got where I once wanted to be, and there was a Maxwell's otter.

It was now early May, and I had been in London for more than three weeks, three weeks of impatience and longing for Camusfeàrna, and I felt I could wait no longer to see Mij playing, as I saw him in my mind's eye, under the waterfall, or free about the burn and the island beaches. I went by way of my family home in the south of Scotland, where Mij could taste a partial but guarded liberty before total freedom in the north.

Travelling with otters is a very expensive business. There was now no question of again confining Mij to a box, and there is, unfortunately, no other legal means of carrying an otter by train. For the illegal means which I followed then and after, I paid, as do all who use black markets, highly. He travelled with me in a first-class sleeper, a form of transport which for some reason he enjoyed hugely; indeed from the very first he seemed to love railway stations, and showed a total disregard for their deafening din and alarming crowd scenes.

At the barrier the railway official punched for me a dog ticket (on which I had noticed the words 'Give full description') and had already turned to the next in the queue before his eyes widened in a perfect double take; then Mij was tugging up the crowded platform at the end of his lead, heedless of the shouts and the bustle, the screaming train hooters and rumbling luggage trolleys.

I had planned the journey with some care; my hush money was already paid; the basket I carried contained everything possibly necessary to Mij for the journey; over my left arm was an army blanket ready to protect the sheets from Mij's platform-grimed paws as soon as he entered the sleeper.

Mij had an instant eye for anything to do with water, and he saw at once that in the wash-basin, however dry at the moment, lay the best chance; he curled up in it, his form fitting its shape as an apple fits a dumpling, and his paws began to fumble with the chromium tap. It was of a type entirely new to him, working by downward pressure, and not a drop could he draw from it for a full five minutes; at last, trying to lever himself into an upright position, he put his full weight on the tap handle and found himself, literally, in his element.

There was only one incident that evening; an

incident, however, that for a moment looked like bringing the whole train to a stop. It had not occurred to me that Mij could, in that very small space, get into any serious mischief; it had not crossed my mind, for example, that by standing on the piled luggage he could reach the communication cord. This, however, was precisely what he had done, and when my eye lit on him he already had it firmly between his teeth while exploring with his paws the tunnel into which its ends disappeared. It was probably nothing but this curiosity as to detail that had so far saved the situation; now as I started towards him he removed his fingers from the hole and braced them against the wall for the tug. It takes a surprisingly strong pull to ring the communication bell, but Mij had the strength, and, it seemed, the will. I caught him round the shoulders, but he kept his grip, and as I pulled him I saw the chain bulge outward; I changed my tactics and pushed him towards it, but he merely braced his arms afresh. Suddenly I knew what to do. Mij was extremely ticklish, particularly over the ribs; I began to tickle him, and at once his jaws relaxed into the foolish grin that he kept for such occasions and he began to squirm. Later that evening he tried several times to reach the cord again, but by then I had rearranged the suitcases, and it was beyond the furtherest stretch of his elastic body.

It was in unfamiliar surroundings such as these

that Mij appeared most often to copy my actions: that night, though by now he had become accustomed to sleep inside the bed with his head to my feet, he arranged himself as he had on the first night at my flat, on his back with his head on the pillow and his arms outside the bedclothes. He was still sleeping like this when the attendant brought my tea in the morning. He stared at Mij, and said 'Was it tea for one, or two, sir?'

During his stay at Monreith, the home of my family, Mij's character began to show itself. At first on farm mill dams, then in the big loch over which the house looks out, and finally in the sea – which, though he had never known salt water, he entered without apparent surprise – he showed not only his amazing swimming powers but his willingness to give up freedom for human company. At first I allowed him to swim only on the end of a long fishing-line, but the danger of underwater snags on which the line might loop itself soon seemed too great, and after the first week he ran free and swam free.

This time of getting to know a wild animal on equal terms, as it were, was fascinating to me, and our long daily walks by stream and hedgerow, moorland and loch, were a source of perpetual delight. Though it remained difficult to lure him from some enticing piece of open water, he was otherwise no more trouble than a dog, and much more interesting to watch. His hunting powers were still not perfect, but he would sometimes corner an eel in the mill dams, and in the streams he would catch frogs, which he skinned with great skill. I found that Mij would follow me through a crowded and cackling farmyard without a glance to right or to left. To most domestic livestock he was indifferent, but black cattle clearly seemed to him to be the water buffaloes of his home, and if they gathered at the edge of water in which he was swimming he became wild with excitement, plunging and porpoising and chittering with pleasure.

Even in the open countryside he kept his passion for toys, and he would carry with him for miles some object that had caught his fancy, a fallen rhododendron blossom, an empty twelve-bore cartridge case, a fir-cone, or, on one occasion, a woman's comb with an artificial brilliant set in the bar; this he discovered at the side of the drive as we set off one morning, and carried it for three hours, laying it down on the bank when he took to water and returning for it as soon as he emerged.

We arrived at Camusfeàrna, my home in the north of Scotland, in early June, soon after the beginning of a long hot spell. That summer at Camusfeàrna seemed to go on and on through time-less hours of sunshine and stillness and the dapple of changing cloud shadow upon the shoulders of the hills.

Into the bright, watery landscape of Camusfeàrna, Mij moved and took possession. The waterfall, the burn, the white beaches and the islands; his form became the familiar foreground to them all – or perhaps foreground is not the right word, for at Camusfeàrna he seemed so absolute a part of his surroundings that I wondered how they could ever have seemed to me complete before his arrival.

At the beginning, Mij's daily life followed something of a routine; this became, as the weeks went on, a total freedom at the centre point of which Camusfeàrna house remained Mij's holt, the den to which he returned at night, and in the daytime when he was tired.

Mij slept in my bed (by now, as I have said, he had abandoned the teddy bear attitude and lay on his back under the bedclothes with his whiskers tickling my ankles and his body at the crook of my knees) and would wake with extraordinary punctuality at exactly twenty past eight in the morning.

His next objective was the eel-box in the burn, followed, having breakfasted, by a tour of the three-quarter circle formed by the burn and the sea; shooting like an under-water arrow after trout where the burn runs deep and slow between the trees; turning over stones for hidden eels where it spreads broad and shallow over the sun-reflecting scales of mica; tobogganing down the long, loose sand slope by the sand-martin colony; diving through the waves on the sand beach and catching dabs; then, lured in with difficulty from starting on a second lap, home to the kitchen and squirming among his towels.

There were great quantities of cattle at Camusfeàrna that year; the majority of them were black, and, as at Monreith in the spring, they seemed to remind Mij of his familiar water buffaloes of the Tigris marshes, for he would dance round them with excited chitterings until they stampeded. After a week or two he invented a means of cattle-baiting at which he became a past master. With extreme stealth he would advance towards the rear end of some massive stirk whose black-tufted tail hung within his reach; then he would grab the tuft between his teeth and give one tremendous jerk upon it with all his strength, leaping backward exactly in time to dodge the lashing hooves. Mij was able to gauge the distance to an inch, and never a hoof so much as grazed him.

I had a book to write during those summer months at Camusfeàrna, and often I would lie for hours in the sun by the waterfall; from time to time Mij would appear from nowhere; with delighted squeaks and gurgles he would rush through the shallows and come bounding up the bank to deposit his skin-load of water upon myself and my manuscript, sometimes adding insult to injury by confiscating my pen as he departed.

In the sea, Mij found his true, breathtaking swimming powers; until he came to Scotland he had never swum in deep waters, for the lakes and lagoons of his native marshes are shallow. Now he would swim beside me as I rowed in the little dinghy, and in the glass-clear waters of Camusfeàrna bay, I could watch him as he dived down, down, down through fathom after fathom to explore the gaudy sea forests at the bottom, with their flowered shell glades and mysterious, shadowed caverns. For hours he would keep pace with the boat, appearing now on this side and now on that, sometimes mischievously seizing an oar with both arms and dragging on it, and from time to time bouncing inboard with a flurry of water.

He caught a number of fish on his daily outings, and in the burn he learned to feel under stones for eels, reaching in with one paw; and I in turn learned to turn over the larger stones for him, so that after a time he would stand in front of some boulder too heavy for him to move, and chitter at me to come and lift it for him.

He loved rough seas too. He rejoiced in the waves; he would hurl himself straight as an arrow right into the great roaring grey wall of an oncoming breaker and go clean through it as if it had neither weight nor momentum; he would swim far out to sea through wave after wave until the black dot of his head was lost among the distant white manes, and more than once I thought that some wild urge to seek new lands had seized him and that he would go on swimming west into the Sea of the Hebrides and that I should not see him again. But though there were anxious times when he was away too long for my peace of mind he always came back.

I returned to London with Mij in the autumn. During the car journey from Camusfeàrna to Inverness he seemed in a long deep sleep, to shed his wild nature and to awake changed into a domestic animal. In the station hotel he lay beside my chair while I had tea, and when a waitress brought him a saucer of milk he lapped it at delicately as any drawing-room cat, spilling never a drop. He entered his first-class sleeper as one long used to travel, and at the studio next morning he seemed actively pleased to be among his old surroundings. He settled quickly, too, into his earlier routine; eels in the bath, and walks round the grubby London streets.

I cannot now remember whether, when I had been in Iraq, I had ever seriously thought what was to be done with an otter during such times as I was unable to look after him myself; when, for example, I was again abroad, or even when I wanted to be

away from my own house for a day or two. Perhaps
I had thought that he could come with me, for I
had not yet learned that an otter is not at its best
as a guest in a strange house – or rather that the
house would be very strange indeed at the end of
the visit. Mij was content to be alone for four or
five hours, but for no longer unless those hours began in the evening, and now I found myself forced
to take the problem seriously.

I began by inserting an advertisement in *Country
Life*, the *Field*, and *The Times*, requesting a temporary home for Mij where he could be left for
anything from days to months as need be. Alto-
gether I received some forty replies, but few of the
writers had any idea of what they would be taking
on; fewer still had premises in any way suitable.
At the end of two months I was no further forward
than on the day I had sent in the advertisement.

Then I began to interview retired zoo keepers,
but a few weeks of this convinced me that a retired
zoo keeper had an implacable intention to remain
retired. Meanwhile the book that I had been writing
was finished, and I should in the normal course of
events have begun to travel. Though I found a temporary solution – to return to Camusfeàrna in the
spring and there to write a book about Mij – these
were clearly no more than delaying tactics, and
with friends in the zoological world I left an urgent
plea to find me, by hook or by crook, a whole-time

otter-keeper. But by the time he was found and engaged, Mij was dead.

What little there remains to tell of this story I
shall write quickly, for anyone who in reading it
has shared a little of my pleasure in his life must
share, too, a little of my unhappiness at his death.

I had arranged to go to Camusfeàrna to spend
the spring and summer alone in his company, and
there to write a book about him. I was to leave London early in April, but I needed a fortnight's
freedom and I arranged that he should go to Scotland before me, in the charge of a friend. I packed
his 'suitcase', a wicker basket full of spare harnesses,
leads, tins of unpolished rice, cod-liver oil, toys half
destroyed but long favoured, and I travelled with
him in the hired car from my flat to Euston station.
It was a big Humber, with a broad ledge between
the top of the back seat and the rear window; here,
I recall with a vividness that is still in some sense
painful, he sprawled upon his back and rolled my
fountain-pen to and fro between his forepaws, or
held it clasped with one of them against his broad,
glossy belly. I called my companion's attention to
the rich sheen of his coat reflecting the neon lights.
He was in his most domesticated mood.

At the station he struggled purposefully at the
lead all the way up the astonished platform to the
sleeper, where he made straight for the wash-basin.

His left hand reached up and fumbled vaguely with the tap. That was the last I ever saw of him.

During the next ten days I received letters telling me of Mij's delight in his freedom, of the fish that he had caught in the river and in the sea; of how he would come in dog-tired and curl up before the fire.

On 16 April I had packed my own luggage, and was to be at Camusfeàrna myself the following afternoon, when I received a telephone call from the estate agent of the property to which Camusfeàrna belonged. It was rumoured, he told me, that an otter had been killed at the village four miles north of Camusfeàrna, and Mij was missing. But the otter that had been killed was said to have been so mangy and scabby that the killer had not thought it worth while to keep the skin. There was no detail.

Nor was there to be any yet; no tidy end, no body to bury at the foot of the rowan tree; no human kindness that would spare to those who had been fond of him the day-long search, the door standing open all through the night.

I got the story little by little. Mij had been wandering widely for some days past, and though he had always returned at night he must have covered great distances, for he had turned up one day at a hamlet some eight miles south by sea. There he had been recognized and gone unharmed; the next day he had journeyed north up the coast to the village where he was killed. Mij had been on his way home when he had met a roadman with a pickaxe, and he had never been taught to fear or distrust any human being. I hope he was killed quickly, but I wish he had one chance to use his teeth on his killer.

He had been with me for a year and a day on the night he had left London.

3

The Coming of Edal

I MISSED Mij desperately, so much that it was a year before I could bring myself to go to Camusfeàrna again. I mourned for my fallen sparrow; he had filled that landscape so completely, had made so much his own every yard of the ring of bright water I loved, that it seemed empty after he had gone from it. I did not stay there after I knew that he was dead; I went abroad, and it was a year before I saw the house again.

I went back in the early spring of 1958 and there, with the cold bright March weather shining on the landscape that had long become my real home, I found myself troubled again by the sadness that I had felt when Mij was killed; dimly at first, and then quite clearly, came the thought that the place was incomplete without an otter, and that there must always be an otter at Camusfeàrna for as long as I lived there.

With the whole world to choose from, I thought it would be quite easy to find another otter, but I was wrong, and for a whole year it was one disappointment after another.

After the last of these I made up my mind to rear

a cub in Scotland. and with that end in view I returned to Camusfeàrna, for a long stay, in the
spring of 1959.

My early inquiries for an otter-keeper had at last
borne fruit, and now I was able to engage Jimmy
Watt, a boy leaving school, who, though without
first-hand knowledge of otters, had a profound
natural feeling for animals and a desire to work
with them. Jimmy came with me.

I had been at Camusfeàrna for no more than a
week when there occurred by far the strangest hap-
pening in the story of my efforts to replace Mijbil,
a coincidence so extraordinary that it may seem to
come out of a fairy-tale.

On 19 April I motored to the station, thirty-odd
miles away, to meet an arriving guest. I arrived
very early in the village, to do some shopping, and
had lunch in the hotel, a large and glossy hotel
that caters for the tourist trade.

I met my guest on the station platform, and we
went back to the hotel for a drink before setting off
for Camusfeàrna. We sat in the sun-lounge that
overlooks the sea, but we were well back from the
window, and out of sight of the gravel sweep beyond the glass. Suddenly the hall porter came running over to us from the hall.

'Mr Maxwell!' he called. 'Mr Maxwell! Come
quick to the door and tell me what's this strange
beast outside – quick!'

I felt an instant certainty of what I was going to see.

Four people were walking past the hotel, making for a car parked near to the jetty. At their heels lolloped a large, sleek otter, of a species that I had never seen, with a silvery-coloured head and a snow-white throat and chest. I had a deep feeling that this could not be real, that I was struggling in a dream.

I rushed up to the party, and began to jabber, probably in a very silly way, about Mijbil and how he had been killed, and about how time and time again my efforts to find a successor had been blocked at the eleventh hour. I must have been talking a great deal, because what they were saying in reply took a long time to sink in, and when it did the sense of dreaming increased almost to the point of giddiness.

'. . . only eight months old and always been free, house-trained, comes and goes as she likes . . . brought her up myself with a bottle. In six weeks we've got to go back to West Africa, so it looked like a zoo or nothing – what else could we do? Everyone admires her, but when they come to the point of actually owning her they all shy off . . . Poor Edal, it was breaking my heart . . .'

We were sitting on the steps of the hotel by this time, and the otter was nuzzling at the nape of my neck – that well-remembered touch of hard whiskers and soft face-fur.

By the time I had taken in what her owners, Dr Malcolm Macdonald and his wife, from Torridon, were saying, the party had dwindled by two; it turned out that the only reason why they had been in the village at all was to give a lift to two foreign girl hikers whose destination it was. And the only reason that I was there was to meet my guest, and the only reason that the Macdonalds and I had met at all was that two hours earlier I had made friends with the hall porter and exchanged stories about people we remembered. I had not sat near enough to the window to see the otter for myself, and if he had not called me they would have passed by the hotel and gone home to Torridon, and I should have finished my drink ten minutes later and gone home to Camusfeàrna.

Ten days later Edal became mine, and there was once more an otter at Camusfeàrna, playing in the burn and sleeping before the hearth.

Malcolm Macdonald has set down for me the circumstances of Edal's early life, and the chain of events that led, on his side, to the strange climax of our meeting, the meeting of the only man in the British Isles who was trying desperately to find a home for a pet otter with the only man who was searching, with equal desperation, for an otter.

She came on the 23rd August, 1958.
For the past year we had been living, my wife Paula

and I, on a mature rubber plantation in the Niger Delta region of West Africa. Our nearest town was Sapele, two miles away and across the Benin river. The house we lived in was old, and built in the rambling barn-like style of half a century ago. It stood in a compound which generations of planters had filled with a profusion of flowering shrubs and fruit trees. We shared it with a motley collection of animal waifs and strays, and in their company we were never lonely.

Paula had been shopping in Sapele that morning, and she came back from the riverside like the Pharaoh's daughter with a little bundle in her arms.

'Just look what I've got!'

The bundle parted and there was a plump broad silvery muzzle spiked with stiff translucent whiskers. Two hazy puppy eyes were struggling to open.

We gazed down on her enraptured and smoothed her velvety coat.

Under the funny flat face a little pink mouth appeared with brand-new needle-points of teeth. It emitted an astonishingly loud demand to be fed. While Paula set off on a frantic rush to collect feeding-bottle and teat, milk and boiled water, I tried to comfort this strange new waif.

In due course the bottle was prepared. Paula took the cub into the crook of her arm and offered her the rubber teat; as soon as she tasted the milk she sucked avidly, but she was soon satisfied, taking little more than an ounce, and fell into a deep contented sleep.

While she slept we took stock of the situation.

At the end of her morning's shopping in Sapele

Mijbil excavating a rotten log in the Monreith woods

Mijbil at the waterfall

Mijbil examining the eel box

Indiarubber fruit and a terrapin shell were amongst Mij's favourite toys

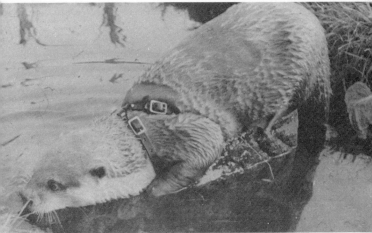

A lost marble

Edal when she first arrived

Lifting a glass net float from the water to play football

Edal about her own pursuits in Camusfeàrna Bay

Edal juggling with a small piece of rubber tube from Schnorkel mask ...

. . . and a silver spoon

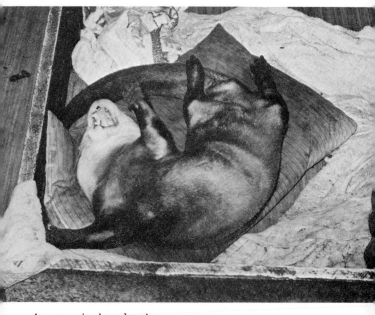

A contortionist asleep!

Opposite and above: Terry and Teko.

The first day with the bathers

Teko sliding down a chute for an eel, seen in mid-air

. . . the ensuing meal

Paula had noticed several Africans standing arguing around one of their number who held a box containing, it seemed to her at first, a couple of very young puppies. Their talk caught her interest.

'Which kind of beef dis?' said one.

'Na tree-bear,' answered another.

'At all,' said a third. 'Dis na rabbit.' (Rabbit is the local name for a species of big rat.) A fourth was emphatic in his disbelief.

'Na lie,' he said.

Paula's curiosity overcame her and she went to see for herself. At the same time a senior African joined the group. 'This be the piccin of water-dog,' he intoned, settling the controversy for good.

Now we had an otter to bring up.

Two hours after her first meal with us she wakened and struggled free of the towel which was her temporary bed. Using her stubby loose-jointed limbs as oars she rowed herself along on her sleek belly. She was pleased to receive our attentions and took another small feed, made up of one part of ordinary canned evaporated milk with two parts of boiled and cooled water added.

In the first two or three weeks she slept most of the time as infants do. She grew rapidly, and almost with every awakening one could see the development of her strength. Movements attracted her; she came to recognize her bottle and would stretch out her hands to hold it.

They were fascinating, those hands. The stubby fingers were strong and mobile and only slightly webbed. Her hands were important to her; she used them to investigate every new object, and as she grew older they developed amazing dexterity.

When feeding, Edal, as we called her, liked to lie on her back in the crook of one's arm. Tightly holding the neck of the bottle she would squirm with pleasure as she sucked, thrusting back hard with her little round head.

As she grew and took on her proper otter shape and became an active member of the household she was delightful. By the end of September she was about eighteen inches long, a scampering, merry little otter cub.

When first introduced to the bath Edal yelled with fright. It took a great deal of talking and soothing to convince her that an otter should like water, but soon she found that it was great fun to splash about in an inch or two of cool water. Not bad stuff to drink, either.

Over a period of days we made her baths gradually deep enough for real swimming. With a supporting hand at first she learned that she could swim. Industriously paddling round she would look up with the most comical expression. 'Well! Just look at me!'

As we laughed at her she positively grinned. 'Wheeeeee.' This was living.

How she loved that bath! She learned to swim under water and do corkscrew rolls. With a thrust of her broad webbed feet she would lunge forward out of the water and belly-flop. She loved, too, to play peek-a-boo over the edge of the bath, diving quick as a flash. She gathered a collection of bath toys, all sorts of odds and ends, though her favourite was a plastic pint measure. First she would sink it; then, drawing a deep breath, she would thrust her head into it and swim with it clattering around the bath.

When she tired she would come to the side to be lifted out and dried. Sometimes she would take over long in tiring and the bath attendant for the occasion would take the plug out. This was an eternal mystery to Edal. Where did that water go? She would thrust her muzzle into the hole, poke her fingers through the grid, sit on it. Finally, the water gone, she would peer wistfully after it and look up inquiringly. Then, accepting the situation with her usual good humour, she would come and be dried.

She loved laughter and would positively join in, grinning and prancing.

Stinky Pooh was one of those starry-eyed fluffy sedate-little-girl kittens who surprise you by behaving like tomboys. She and Edal would roll and tumble in ferocious mock battles, and their greatest joy was a friendly squabble over a ball of screwed-up paper.

The grey parrot we had wasn't really a playmate. A glutton for petting himself, he was jealous of the little stranger. He had come to us as 'dash' – pidgin English for a present – and, not knowing at first that he was a cock bird, we called him Polly. As the youngsters roistered on the floor Polly would watch them with his pale cold eyes. Like a crotchety old Giles schoolmaster he would hobble across the room and, pecking them indiscriminately, would take away their paper ball.

Carrying it to his perch by the window he would moodily tear it to shreds.

Poor Polly; when Edal grew a little older Polly met his deserts. One day he fled squawking while she, munching on a mouthful of red tail feathers, registered sheer delight.

The diet we gave her seemed satisfactory, for she grew well, and was always bursting with high good humour. Nothing escaped her interest, and everything was examined for its possibilities as a plaything. Bottles were just made to be rolled upon and a box of matches was treasure-trove. She appeared to derive enormous satisfaction from scattering a boxful of matches and then packing them, one by one, into the toe of a slipper. Finally she would thrust her arm through the cover of the box and wear it like an outsize bangle. All this made life pretty lively when I settled down to relax with a drink and cigarettes at night.

Her appetite was astounding. She took a great interest in our own meals and attended regularly at the table for titbits. She rejected all cooked meats except pork and ham, liked some vegetables, especially runner beans, enjoyed pastry, and was frantically fond of ice-cream. She would take a piece in both hands and cram it into her mouth, making ecstatic little mewing noises and getting thoroughly messy. When offered a tasty morsel she really wanted she would moan softly and 'hurrrh' through her nose before taking it.

She drank frequently and spent a great deal of her time in the bathroom, for when not actually in the bath she liked to take her day-time naps there. She liked a towel to sleep on, and if one were not already provided she would help herself, pulling one down from the towel-rail and dragging it off to a quiet corner. Bunching it up beneath her she would worry at it until she found a suitable part to suck; then she would suck at it with tremendous fervour, eyes shut tight, mewing and snuffling and waggling her rump until she fell asleep.

The New Year came, and we began to be anxious for her future. We were due to return to the United Kingdom at the beginning of March, and although several kind people offered to keep her we hated the thought of abandoning her. She was still very young and she was deeply attached to us, as indeed we were to her. At that time we were half-persuaded that the best eventual home for her would be a good zoo, where she would receive the best of care from professional animal keepers, but we have since been sadly disillusioned on that score.

One afternoon I was to meet Paula at the Sapele ferry. Edal followed me to the car so I took her along with some idea of accustoming her to travelling. At first she was nervous in the car, clinging anxiously to my neck and pressing hard against me. I drove slowly down to the waterside, talking to her all the while, and persuading her that she had nothing to fear.

We sat waiting near to the ferry pier, at peace with the world. An African girl with a basket of peppers on her head sauntered by singing.

As she saw Edal the basket teetered and her eyes dilated wide. She yelled.

'Yah! Look um! Look de beef!'

In seconds a jabbering crowd surrounded us.

'Eh! Look um!'

'Look 'e'n teeth!'

'Dem pass dog own!'

' 'E fit to bite man proppah!'

'How 'e no de bite white man?'

'Ah! Dis na docitah. I t'ink say 'e gie um injection.'

A seamy faced character in tattered shorts, evidently a fisherman, pushed into the crowd.

'Eh Heh! Na watta-dog! 'E keel feesh fo' watta! 'E bad fo' we! If 'e get a chance 'e savvy bite man too much!'

I had started the engine, and as I let in the clutch our knowledgeable friend was expounding the culinary properties of young otters.

'As 'e dead now, 'e sweet to chop ...'

It was decided that Edal should come with us, and we had a long and difficult journey from Africa to Scotland.

At Inverness the morning was crisp and bright. I took delivery of my car at the station and we headed for the country, pausing only to buy some fish for her. The day was fine and clear with the warmth of spring in the air, and we dawdled along towards the mountains of the western seaboard, revelling in the pastel highland hues after Africa's garish colours, and stopping often to let Edal investigate her new homeland. She was happy to be free with us again, and bore us no ill will for the horrors of the journey. She travelled well by car but was a restless passenger, scrambling from side to side to peer out of the windows.

In the next few weeks, as the spring unfolded, I explored anew with Edal the sea-shore and the mountain burns that I had known in my childhood. Although she recoiled at first from the biting chill of the water, our colder climate seemed to agree with her. On the ebb tides we dug the succulent clams from the sands and she learned to hunt for crabs and cobbler-fish among the rocks and tangle.

Those were happy weeks indeed, but we were due to go to Ghana in June and again we began to worry about her future. Dearly as we loved to have her with us, the necessity for many more thousands of miles of travel made parting with her, at least for a time, inevitable. We were anxious to see her properly settled and in good hands before the time came for us to go.

One beautiful morning in late April we set out to motor to the village of Plockton, near Kyle of Lochalsh. For most of the previous evening we had discussed what we might best do for Edal, and were miserable at the prospect of parting with her. We had been urged to lodge her in a particular zoo, and had been assured she would be given every care and attention there. Still we recoiled from the idea, and could reach no decision.

On the road to Plockton two foreign girls on a youth hostelling holiday hitched a lift with us. They wanted to go to Skye, and since the ferry was but a few miles off our route we elected to take them there.

We made our usual intermittent progress, stopping

every twenty miles or so to let Edal out for a while. In the early afternoon we stopped at the Lochalsh Hotel and wandered along the terrace, looking across to the hills of Skye. The gods were smiling on us that day, for they had taken the nagging question of Edal's future into their own hands. As we came abreast of the hotel door a figure bolted from it like a ferreted rabbit, laying a trail of whisky from the glass clutched forgotten in his hand, his whole attention fixed delightedly and incredulously on Edal.

4

Edal at Camusfeàrna

NOTHING was decided at that first meeting; Edal's owners not unnaturally wanted to satisfy themselves that this extraordinary coincidence was all it seemed, and that she would find with me the home they wanted for her. They promised to write during the next few days; Edal jumped into their car with the ease of familiarity, and as they drove away she appeared, leaning far out of the passenger window, one hand delicately shielding her windward ear.

A week later she visited Camusfeàrna for an afternoon; then, after an interval of ten days Malcolm and Paula came to stay for a week-end, to leave Edal with me when they went. I had not been idle during those ten days; I was determined to repeat none of the mistakes that had led, directly or indirectly, to Mij's death. I sent to Malcolm Macdonald a harness that had been made for Mij just before he was killed; with the help of Jimmy Watt I enclosed the house with a fence that might not have foiled Mij, but which would, I thought, be barrier enough to baffle Edal if she should think in the first days to seek her late foster parents; within these confines

57

we dug a pool and piped to it water that rose in a fountain jet.

Even during that first week-end, while I was still a stranger to her and her surroundings were unfamiliar, I was so enchanted by Edal that I found it difficult to believe my own good fortune. I knew that if I had searched the world over I could have found no more perfect successor to Mijbil.

On the third day, while Edal was sleeping soundly on the sofa, Paula and Malcolm left silently. Our good-byes were hushed, both because we did not want to awaken that softly breathing ball of fur, and because I shared something of their own feeling of unhappiness and betrayal, and in my long-postponed moment of triumph I felt sadness for the sundered family.

After they had gone Jimmy and I sat beside Edal on the sofa, waiting miserably for her awakening and the panic that we thought would follow the realization of her abandonment. An hour passed, two, and still she slept on. We sat silently and anxiously, as around a sick bed, and my thoughts wandered between the sleeping animal and her late owners; for nothing in the world would I have changed places with them as they drove home desolate now.

When Edal awoke at last she appeared to notice little amiss. Paula's jersey lay beside her on the sofa,

her own towel and toys were on the floor, and if she
was aware of her owners' absence she was too well-
mannered a guest to comment upon it so early.

It is time to give a more detailed description of
Edal as she was when she came to me early in May
1959.

By far the strangest and most charming aspect of
her was that of her hands. Unlike Mij's, whose
forepaws were true paws with wide connecting webs
between the fingers, hers were monkey-hands, un-
webbed, without so much as a trace of nail, and
nearly as mobile as a man's. With them she ate,
peeled hard-boiled eggs, picked her teeth, arranged
her bed, and played for hours with any small object that she could find.

Once in a hospital in Italy I watched a cripple
child practising the use of artificial hands. She
had before her a solitaire board and a numbered
set of marbles; the holes were numbered too, but
the marbles had been wrongly placed, and her task
was to transpose them until each ball and socket
corresponded. She worked with complete absorp-
tion, oblivious of onlookers, and with each passing
minute she discovered new powers. Once, too, I
had watched a ball juggler practising his act with
the same withdrawn, inturned eye, the same absence of irritation or impatience at failure, the
same apparent confidence of final success.

Of both of these Edal reminded me as she jug-
gled with such small objects – marbles, clothes-
pegs, matches, Biro pens – as could be satisfactorily
contained within her small, prehensile grasp; she
would lie upon her back passing them from hand
to hand, or occasionally to the less adept grip of
her webbed but almost nail-less hind feet, working
always with two or more objects at a time, gazing
fixedly at them all the while, as though these hands
and feet of hers were in some way independent of
her and to be watched and wondered at. She would
retrieve a lost marble clutching it firmly in one
hand – usually the right – and hobbling along
upon her other three limbs.

Because, it seemed, of her delight in her own
dexterity, it was her practice to insert her plaything
of the moment into some container from which it
had then to be taken out, a boot or a shoe for
choice, and it mattered little to her whether this
already contained a human foot. She would come
hobbling across the room to me with some invisible
treasure clenched in her right fist and thrust it into
my shoe below the ankle-bone; on more than one
occasion the foreign body thus introduced turned
out to be a large and lively black beetle. She was
also a clever, if not an entirely stealthy, pickpocket;
with impatiently fumbling fingers she would reach
into the trouser-pockets of any guest who sat down
in the house, hardly waiting for an introduction

before scattering the spoils and hurrying away with as much as she could carry. With these curious hands she could, too, throw such playthings as were small enough to be enclosed by her fingers. She had three ways of doing this; the most usual was a quick upward flick of the arm and forepart of the body as she held her clenched fist palm downward, but she would also perform a backward flick which tossed the object over her shoulder to land at her other side, and, on occasion, usually when in a sitting position with her back supported, she would throw overarm.

Like Mij, she was an ardent footballer, and would dribble a ball round the room for half an hour at a time, but here she had something that Mij had not learned, for when she shot the ball wide or overran it she would sweep her broad tail round with a powerful scoop to bring it back within range of her feet.

For the rest she was a small, exceedingly heavy body living inside a rich fur skin many sizes too large for her. It cannot be described as a loose fit; it is not a fit at all. The skin appears to be attached to the creature inside it at six points only: the base of the nose, the four wrists or ankles, and the root of the tail. When lying at ease upon her back the surplus material may be observed in heavy velvety folds at one or other side of her, or both; a slight pressure forward from the base of her neck causes the skin on her forehead to rise in a mountain of pleats like a furled plush curtain; when she stands upright like a penguin the whole garment slips downwards by its own weight into heavy wrinkles at the base of her belly, giving her a non-upsettable, pear-shaped appearance.

Her comparative babyhood, and her upbringing by human beings, had left some strange gaps in her abilities. To start with, she could not lap water or milk, but could only drink from a dish as does a bird, lifting her head to allow the liquid to trickle down her throat, or sucking it noisily with a coarse, soup-drinking sound punctuated with almost vocal swallowing. She possessed, however, an accomplishment probably unchallenged among wild animals – that of drinking milk from a spoon. One had but to produce and exhibit a cup and spoon for her to clamber on to one's lap and settle herself with a heavy and confiding plump, head up and expectant. Then she opened her mouth and one poured the spoonfuls into it, while the soup noises reached a positive crescendo. At the end of this performance she would insist upon inspecting the cup to make certain that it was indeed empty; she would search into it with inquiring fingers and abstracted gaze; then, belching and hiccuping from time to time, she would lift the spoon out in one clenched hand and lie upon her back, licking and sucking it.

It came as a shock to me to discover that she was

the most uncertain of swimmers. Even in the wild state otter cubs have little if any instinct for water, and their dam teaches them to swim against their better judgement, as it were, for they are afraid to be out of their depth. In the water Edal preferred to keep her feet either in surreptitious contact with the bottom or within easy reach of it, and nothing, at that time, would tempt her into deep water. Within these self-imposed limits, however, she was capable of a performance that even Mij might have envied; lying on her back she would begin to spin, if this is the correct word, to revolve upon her own axis like a chicken on a spit that has gone mad. In this, as in the novelty of new aquabatic powers that she quickly learned, she took a profound delight, and if she had not yet realized that otters should swim under-water and only return to the surface for refreshment, she knew all the joys of a great disturbance upon it.

At the end of a fortnight there was no further danger of her straying. We had provided her with so many distractions, so many novelties – and the greatest of these was certainly constant access to running water – that she had been won over. It was, perhaps, fortunate for us that this period coincided with the migration of the elvers. For these transparent morsels, who swarmed and wriggled in the rock pools below the waterfall and formed a broad snail-paced queue up the vertical rock beside the white water, she discovered a passion that obscured every other interest. Hour after hour she would pass about these pools where Mij had hunted before her, scooping and pouncing, grabbing and munching, reached up the rock face to pluck the pilgrims as they journeyed, and from these lengthy outings she would return surfeited to play and to sleep in the kitchen as if she had known no other home.

She had her breakfast of live eels, sent, as they had been for Mij, from London, and then one or other of us took her for a two-hour walk along the shore or over the hills. During these walks she would remain far closer at hand than Mij had done, and we carried the lead not so much as a possible restraint upon her as a safeguard against attack by one of the shepherds' dogs, for Edal loved dogs, regarded them as her playmates, and was quite unaware that many dogs in the Western Highlands are both encouraged and taught to kill otters.

In the rock pools along the shore Edal learned to catch gobies and butter-fish; occasionally she would corner a full-grown eel in the hill streams, and little by little she discovered the speed and powers of her race. Her staple diet was of eels sent alive from London, for probably no otter can remain entirely healthy without eels, but she was also fond of ginger nuts, bacon fat, butter, and other whimsical *hors d'œuvre* to which her upbringing by humans had accustomed her. Among local fish she disdained the saithe or coal fish, tolerated lythe and trout, and would gorge herself gluttonously upon mackerel. We put her eels alive into her pool, where after early failures in the cloud of mud that her antics stirred up, she proved able to detect and capture them even in the midst of that dense smoke-screen.

By the end of June she was swimming as an otter should, diving deep to explore dim rock ledges at the edge of the sea tangle, remaining for as much as two minutes under water, so that often only a thin track of bubbles from the imprisoned air in her fur gave guide to her whereabouts. But though she lost her fear of depth she never felt secure in great spaces of water; she liked to see on at least one side of her the limits of the element as she swam, and when she could not she would panic into an infantile and frenzied dog-paddle as she raced for land.

Hence our first experiments with her in the rowing-boat were not a success. The boat was to her clearly no substitute for terra firma, and in it, on deep water, she felt as insecure as if she were herself overboard – more so, in fact, for she would brave a wild rush for the shore rather than remain with us in so obvious a peril.

From the last days of May until early September

the summer, that year, took leave of absence; while
England panted in the heat and the coast roads
from London were jammed by twenty-mile queues
of motionless cars, Camusfeàrna saw only sick
gleams of sunshine between the ravings of gale and
rain; the burn came down in roaring spate, and the
sea was restless under the unceasing winds. The
bigger dinghy dragged her moorings and stove a
plank, and there were few days when the little flat-
bottomed pram could take the sea without danger.
Because of this, and because, perhaps, I welcomed
Edal's fear of the open sea as a factor in favour of
her safety, it was not until the first of September
that we renewed experiments with her in the
boats.

She had gained much confidence meanwhile,
both in us and in her proper element, and she
gambolled round us in the warm sunshine as we
dragged the pram across the sand into a still blue
sea that reflected the sky without so much as a
ripple. Edal shot through the clear, bright sea,
grabbing and clasping the oar blades or bouncing
inboard with a flurry of aerated water, as we rowed
for a mile down the coastline, with the glorious
ochres and oranges of tide-bared weed as a foreground to the heather, reddening bracken, and the
blue distances of mountain heights. All the magic
of Camusfeàrna was fixed in that morning; the
vivid lightning streak of an otter below water;

the long, lifting, blue swell of the sea among the skerries and the sea tangle; the little rivers of froth and crystal that spilled back from the rocks as each smooth wave sucked back and left them bare.

Edal, finding herself from time to time swimming above an apparently bottomless abyss, would still panic suddenly and rush for the boat in a racing dog-paddle, her head above water and not daring to look down; her instinctive memories, it seemed, alternated between those of the dim mysterious depth and forests of waving weed, and the security of the hearthrug, lead, and reassuring human hands. So she would turn suddenly for the boat (of which she had now lost all fear and felt to be as safe as the dry land), a small anxious face above furiously striking forefeet, cleaving the surface with a frothing arrow of wave, and leap aboard with her skin-load of water. Then she would poise herself on the gunwale, webbed hind feet gripping tensely, head submerged, peering down on the knife edge between sea and terra firma, between the desire for submarine exploration and the fear of desertion in the deep unknown. Sometimes she would slide, soundlessly and almost without ripple, into deep water, only to panic as soon as she had submerged and strike out again frantically for the boat. Yet in the moments when her confidence had not yet deserted her, when the slim torpedo of her form glided deep below the boat's side, weaving over the white sand between tall, softly-waving trees of bright weed, or darting in sudden swift pursuit of some prey invisible from above, it seemed as if the clock had been set back and it was Mijbil who followed the dinghy through the shining water.

The house had been much changed since Edal's arrival. While there had been no otter at Camus-feàrna I had been trying to improve the décor and comfort of the rooms; now that the whole premises were once more, as it were, in a state of siege this had to be abandoned for more practical considerations. Every table and shelf had somehow to be raised above the range of Edal's inquisitive fingers; every hanging object upon the walls moved upward like the population of a flooded town seeking safety upon the rooftops. No longer could there be a paper-table at the end of the sofa, for this recently constructed improvement she took for her own on the first day, tearing and crumpling all that silly print until it formed a bed suited to her exacting taste. There she lay upon her back and slept, her head pillowed across a headline describing traffic jams on the roads out of London.

It was exceedingly difficult to elevate every object above her reach, for by standing on tiptoe she could already achieve three foot six inches. When wet she would pull down a towel, or several towels, upon which to dry herself; when bored she would possess herself of any object that caught her fancy, and set about its destruction. These moods would come and go; there were days when she was as sedate as a lap-dog, but there were days, too, when there simply was not room enough on the walls for the fugitives from her.

Because of the lack of wall space in the kitchen-living-room it was not advisable to leave Edal quite alone there for long periods. She was less demanding in this matter of being left alone than Mij had been, and if she had been exercised and fed she was content for five hours or more. When we went by boat to the village or over to Skye we would leave her shut into a room given up entirely to her, the unfurnished room over the kitchen, that had served the same purpose in Mij's day. Here she had her bed, made from a motor tyre covered with rugs; her lavatory in a corner, composed of news-papers laid on American cloth (to this somewhat remote convenience she would dutifully ascend from the kitchen whenever necessary); a host of miscellaneous toys; and dishes of water. This room had one great disadvantage; it had a single-plank floor and it was directly above the living room. Though her water bowls were of the non-upsettable variety made for dogs, they were far from non-

upsettable to her, for having tried and failed to tip
them by leverage she would simply pick them up
in both hands and overturn them; and the ceiling
was, as I have indicated, far from waterproof. Water
multiplies its value to an otter as soon as it is falling or otherwise on the move, and Edal discovered
that having overturned her bowl upstairs it was
possible to scamper down to the kitchen and receive the double dividend of the drops falling
through the ceiling; I have seen her on the kitchen
floor, head up and mouth wide open, catching
every drip as it pattered down from above.

It was a source of great disappointment to Edal
that the few dogs she was allowed to meet fell far
short of her standards as playmates. In general their
attitude towards her reminded me of nothing so
much as the colour-bar, and she clearly felt hurt
at their failure to accept her as one of themselves.
With few exceptions they growled, barked, and
snarled at her overtures. The first, a sedate Golden
Labrador bitch, sat in front of the fire with her
back turned to Edal in a most marked manner;
every now and again Edal, discouraged from more
direct approach by an unequivocal snap, would ten-
tatively stretch out one of her monkey-like hands
and touch the unresponsive yellow rump, making,
the while, little plaintive, yearning whines in the
back of her throat. She was plainly puzzled by her

failure to establish relations, for she was unused to rebuff.

Two dogs only achieved with her a temporary *bonhomie*, but both, after a short time, found her personality too overpowering. A peculiarly zany, yellow-eyed pointer bitch, brought over by James Robertson Justice, entered to begin with into the true spirit that Edal required of her playmates, racing round and round in dazzling circles while Edal displayed remarkable judgement in the matter of short cuts – too remarkable for the pointer, who ended upon her back in the burn while Edal mocked her from the bank. This incident produced a coolness that their relationship did not survive; the pointer became wary and then frankly hostile. When I expostulated at this deplorable lack of stamina her owner replied, 'Well, she never thought she was going to be called upon to make sport for an otter, least of all one called Crumpet.' (Like most curious pets Edal had, since her arrival at Camusfeàrna, acquired a variety of alternative names, among which this was perhaps one of the least regrettable.)

Eric Linklater introduced a great rangy English setter, a gorgeous beast named Tops'l, and he, too, was at first prepared to chance his arm playing with an otter, this time on the sand; but like the pointer, he found his ability to make rings round her set at nought by her unerring eye for radii. Thus consistently outwitted, he took refuge in hysterical barking, and Edal took refuge in the sea. I still hope some time to find a dog who will play with her properly, but by now her teeth are perhaps too sharp for a dog's skin.

5

Edal and Teko

WHEN I went to North Africa in the early winter
Edal came to London with her keeper Jimmy Watt
– and seemed to resent her changed circumstances
as little as Mij had done in the past. She had a
room of her own with a door to the garden and a
large glass tank, and she had the huge selection of
toys which is one of the things necessary to keep
an otter contented. While I was abroad I used to
receive news of her whenever I was within reach of
mail and I looked forward on my return to taking
her back to Camusfeàrna and to renewed freedom.

I came back from North Africa in the early
spring. I had come straight from the nightmare
ruins of Agadir, a prosperous city reduced by earth-
quake in a matter of minutes to a place of death
and dust, and all this in a temperature of 105° in
the shade. I thought I knew what I was coming
home to, and I was a little sad because of it. A week
earlier news had reached me from England that
there had been a fire in my London home, and that
in the course of it the tropical birds that I had kept
free in my sitting-room had all died. These birds

73

had been tame and confiding, and when I was sitting at my writing desk I used to love to see them stretch their jewelled wings in free flight about the room and listen to their joyous voices.

But the fire had been on one floor only, and Edal, who occupied a basement room leading into the garden, had slept through it undisturbed, thinking, perhaps, that the noises above her head were some tiresome human prank of no concern to her.

I had expected a riotous welcome from her, but when I walked into the room and spoke her name she barely lifted her head. At first I thought that she was sleepy and had not recognized me; only slowly did I understand that she was very ill. It had begun, I learned, a short time before, with drowsiness and loss of appetite; a vet had called and had not taken a serious view. But now she had not touched food for two days and took little interest in her surroundings. It was clear to me that she was a very sick animal.

Veterinary tests showed that she had more than one disease, and in the end so little is known about otters that it was difficult to know which was the more dangerous and which we ought to treat first. For a fortnight it was touch-and-go. She was losing strength very quickly, and as she would eat nothing we had forcibly to feed her with concentrated liquids. Every day Jimmy and I had to take her by car to the surgery for no less than three injections, for we had found that she resented these painful indignities less, and became more manageable, when she was in strange surroundings. For what seemed a very long time there was little change; at best she had a fifty-fifty chance of living, and though we tempted her with every kind of dainty she would eat nothing of her own will. Then one morning I noticed, as we drove down the King's Road on our daily visit to the surgery, that she seemed for the first time to be taking a little of her old interest in the traffic and the passers-by; she even climbed up as she used to and peered a little short-sightedly out of the passenger's window. In the surgery she was restless, and eyed the vet with distinct disfavour. He looked at her and said 'I do believe we've done the trick. This morning she really looks like an animal that's going to live.' The same afternoon I opened her door quietly, and found her engaged in guzzling a plate of scrambled eggs, stuffing her mouth full with those curious little monkey-like hands just as she used to. It was the first solid food she had eaten for sixteen days. From then on she made a steady recovery; by 14 April she was her usual high-spirited self and greeted a TV unit with all her old enthusiasm for novelties. A few days later we travelled up to Camusfeàrna for the summer.

But in the meantime had taken place a further one of those coincidences that make my experiences with otters read like fiction rather than fact. To appreciate the extent of the coincidence it should be understood that the West African species of otter to which Edal belongs has very rarely been brought to this country at all, and never, so far as I know, had there been a specimen bottle-reared from blind helplessness as Edal had been by Dr Malcolm Macdonald. Now, a short time before I left London with Edal, there was a telephone call, an appointment made, and there sitting outside my door was a car containing an entrancing male cub of the same species, bottle-reared in Sierra Leone by Mr and Mrs Davin who were on short leave in the U.K. It was Edal's story all over again, repeated just a year later. I did not want to bring Teko, as the cub was called, into the house, for fear that there might still be some trace of Edal's infection; this was doubly important, as his owners explained to me, for not only did he eat with his fingers as Edal did, but he also had a baby habit of sucking them. Mr Davin reached into the car and came out with a superb ball of chocolate-coloured plush which in his arms uncoiled and reformed as an otter lying on its back. It put three fingers of its right hand into its mouth and began to suck noisily, looking around it with interest. This otter seemed even more puppy-like than Edal had been. It was the hour when the local school empties, and the children began to crowd round, screaming and laughing, the bolder ones

trying to touch him. Most animals, and more particularly most wild animals, would be upset by this
sort of thing, but Teko greeted them all happily,
and was clearly dying to be allowed to play with
them. Already in my mind's eye I could see Teko
and Edal gambolling together under the waterfall
at Camusfeàrna or porpoising after each other in
the calm bay below the house; already I was mentally enlarging the size of the otter bed in the cot-
tage kitchen. Teko had not been offered to me, but
I knew that before they went back to Sierra Leone
his owners would want to find a home for him, and
I knew that few households were allowed to revolve
round the life of otters as was mine. When I
learned that Mr and Mrs Davin intended anyway
to visit the West Highlands during their holiday,
bringing Teko with them, I felt that the warmth
of his welcome would be so great both from humans
and from Edal as to leave his owners no room for
choice about his future. But I reckoned without
Edal's highly developed sense of property.

Edal returned with me to the West Highlands
and revelled anew in the freedom of the stream and
the sea and the fair golden weather that seems never
to desert Camusfeàrna for long; it seemed to be
the beginning of just such another summer idyll as
the last – but it was not.

In due course Mr and Mrs Davin arrived with
Teko, who was obviously delighted by the breadth

of these new country surroundings, and we made
our first careful attempts at introducing him to
Edal. I am thankful that we took as many pre-
cautions as we did, for otherwise I think there
would have been little left of Teko after the first
five minutes. A year before, when Edal first arrived,
any other animal was a welcome playmate; then, I
am sure, she would have taken Teko to her heart
with joy. But by now I had a faint suspicion that
jealousy and possessiveness played a part in her
make-up, and I felt that this first meeting should be
very carefully arranged. Teko waited on the end of
a lead held firmly by his owners, at some distance
from the house, while I brought Edal out, also on
her lead. At first she did not see him; she saw the
strangers, and she stood on her hind legs like a
penguin to get a better view, for otters are very
short-sighted and trust far more to their noses than
to their eyes. Then she advanced a few paces and
stood up again. She was no more than ten or fifteen
yards from the group, and this time she saw Teko.
Her nostrils wiggled furiously and she caught a
whiff of his scent – then she let out a scream of pure
anger and made a dash for him that almost pulled
me off my feet. It was not an encouraging start.
For a quarter of an hour we walked the two otters
along the beach and about the field, always at a res-
pectful distance from each other, while Edal kept
up a running commentary of piercing rage. Then I

took her back into the house, and Teko's owners and I conferred as generals confer when they find that they are attacking an unassailable position. At length it seemed to us that the place of their meeting might have something to do with it, and that she might perhaps accept him if it were to take place on neutral ground over which Edal did not feel herself to reign supreme. So the following day we tried again some miles away, but after two such attempts it was clear that wherever she might be she felt herself to be monarch of all she surveyed. On the third day there seemed to be a slight improvement; her penetrating song of hatred was not quite so continuous, but she was, I think, consciously lulling us into a sense of false security. She was walking quite silently a few paces behind Teko – she had in fact been silent for quite five minutes – when he lagged a little behind his owners' heels and gave her the opportunity for which she had been waiting so patiently. With a shriek and a single bound she had him by the tail and was worrying it like a dog trying to kill a rat. I managed to haul her off almost as it happened and Teko fled whimpering pathetically to the consoling hands of his foster parents while Edal went into a positive paean of hate and triumph. There seemed nothing that we could do, and the following day I watched Teko's departure with a profound disappointment. I wanted him very much, but I could see no way to solve the problem Edal had set us, for Camusfeàrna is a small house, and it would have required much work to provide separate quarters for another otter. Time was short and Teko's owners were wasting their leave; meanwhile they were to occupy my London house, with its special otter quarters, while they looked for a suitable home for him. But suitable homes for otters are not easy to find, and it was no real surprise to me when a little over a fortnight later they telephoned to ask how long it would take me to prepare separate quarters for Teko.

In the end we had to do it in a week, and a very hard week's work it was, though fortunately most of the materials were to hand. I had expected that after my book about Camusfeàrna was published more and more uninvited visitors would find their way to the house, and visualizing that these might be accompanied by dogs unfriendly to otters I had decided to enclose a piece of land round the house with a continuous five-foot-high wooden paling, with double gates. The planking for this formidable undertaking had been delivered by sea and now lay on the beach below the house. We decided to begin by making with this material a separate enclosure for Teko at one end of the house, where was also a lean-to outhouse that might be converted to his use. Storage space has always been a problem at Camusfeàrna and the contents of this building had long since become a jumble of lobster pots, ropes,

tins, and every imaginable junk, to say nothing of
the uneven layer of coal waste that covered the
few visible parts of the floor. Teko was an animal
accustomed to living in human houses, and to lodge
him in something that did not resemble a human
room would have been as inappropriate as to chain
a drawing-room pekinese to a barrel full of straw.
In that week, then, we had to reclaim, repaint and
furnish the outhouse, make a sizeable enclosure
leading from it, to dig and cement a pool, and to
lead running water to it. With these basic conditions
as his background, Teko could then come into the
kitchen at any time that Edal was in her own room,
and he could accompany us for walks or swims behind the boats when she had had her usual two
hours' morning exercise. Admittedly keeping the
two otters looked like being a full-time job, but,
as someone remarked, it was perhaps as good a
way of earning a living as any other.

Somehow we managed to complete all this work
in the week at our disposal, and though the cement
was still damp enough to take the imprint of Teko's
feet as he entered, and the paint was barely dry upon
the walls of his house, he appeared entranced with
his new quarters. He registered absolute approval
in every way that an otter can, and never once did
he whimper or call or behave otherwise than as if
the place had always been his home. For the first
few nights I put a camp bed in his house and slept

there myself, for sharing sleeping quarters with an animal is one of the most certain ways of getting him used to a stranger. It was not an entirely comfortable procedure, for he had a habit of exploring one's face with those monkey-like hands, pushing his mobile fingers between one's lips, up one's nostrils and into one's ears, but after half an hour or so of this he would squirm down into the warmth of the sleeping bag and sleep until morning. Or so I had thought, but on the third morning I found that he had spent the greater part of the night chewing holes in the material, so that I awoke to find myself engulfed in a smother of liberated kapok, blocking my nose, eyes and ears.

Teko was a weighty ball of dark-brown fur and fat and good humour, as bouncy as a Boxer puppy and as soft as velvet. In character he is like neither Mijbil nor Edal, for he is basically a clown. In a year he has grown to be the biggest otter that I personally have seen, but in moments of meditation he still lies upon his back and sucks his fingers like a baby. For the rest, he is full of *joie de vivre*; he will play for hours with the dancing beam of a torch upon a shadowed floor, executing the while a jig-step that has come to be known as the *pas de loutre*; he will ride a swimmer's back in the sea and dive as the swimmer dives, or porpoise round and round him with the rhythmic grace of a ballet dancer; he seems to laugh at his own antics and at those of all the world around him. Alas, Edal's only reaction to him remained one of violent jealousy against an interloper. Like the Marquis of Montrose, her heart did evermore disdain a rival to her throne, and after those first experiments it was clear that she would kill him were she given the opportunity. But if Edal has refused to accept him as her consort he is yet a king otter in his own right.

When Teko was plainly settled into his new home we tried again to introduce him to Edal. Part of our difficulty lay in the fact that we did not know whether Edal had a greater affection for her keeper, Jimmy Watt, or for myself, and so we did not know who should lead which animal. Nor did her behaviour do much to make this problem easier; she was furious if either of us led Teko, and she was even more furious if he stopped for a second to pick up some shell or piece of jetsam that struck him as a desirable toy. But as the weeks passed I began to have some hope; her attention was not always fixed upon him, nor, when we separated and our respective otters were let off the leads, did she seem inclined to follow Teko and put him to rout.

Nevertheless it was a difficult enough situation, for having to exercise them separately took up a great deal of time, and otters have to be played with besides exercised. I found myself getting far behind with my real work, which is writing books. So we decided on a second otter-keeper, and in July Terry

Nutkins arrived from London. His real interest was in elephants, but he liked all animals, and I could see in the first hour he and Teko were going to become friends. Furthermore, he was a stranger to Edal, so she could not be jealous about his leading Teko.

Then, early in August, all experiments stopped together, for it became not a question of whether we could save this situation but whether we could save Edal's life. Edal, who had for so long played marbles with us on the kitchen floor, slept on our pillows, and displayed all the intense affection of which an otter is capable, developed an infection of the brain arising from a septic tooth. In twenty-four hours she became a mad, savage, half paralysed but unapproachable creature, recognizing no one, as dangerous as a wounded leopard yet to me as pathetic as a child mortally sick. I can still see her crazed head weaving in search of something to attack, her useless hindquarters dragging before she would collapse into a twitching rigor. Perhaps I may not be blamed too much for having hoped that each of these might be the end of an animal that now bore no resemblance to Edal.

6

Grief and the Happy Ending

It had started, as I have said, with a septic tooth, and as soon as we saw that she was in pain we arranged to have the tooth extracted the next day. This meant taking her to a far-distant town, and as always happens on such occasions the next day was Sunday. The vet was, however, prepared to perform the operation at any time, and early in the morning we set off up the hill on foot, for there is no road to my house. At this stage Edal seemed normal, though once or twice it struck me fleetingly that there were moments when she found balance difficult. This suggested that something was affecting the part of her brain responsible for controlling movement, and with my very small knowledge it seemed wise to take some precaution against the possibility of a similar disturbance of the forebrain, responsible for behaviour; so I insisted that Jimmy Watt should wear thick gloves before trying to get her into the car. This was a Land-Rover, with a division between front and rear, and we made up a bed for her on the middle seat in front, so that she was between us. Trouble started within the first half-mile. Without any warning she flew at Jimmy's hands, and if they had not been heavily gloved the damage would have been considerable. Again and again she repeated this, and I thought my own ungloved hands would be her next target, for she seemed to resent movement, and I had to reach directly in front of her in order to use the gear lever. But in her muzzy brain it was Jimmy that she hated at that moment, and she treated me as though I did not exist. At the end of three miles it was clear that the situation was impossible, and that one or other of us would get seriously hurt long before we had completed the eighty miles before us. In the state she was in it was not easy to see how to get her into the rear compartment, much less close the door on her, and it seemed an age before we at last succeeded.

At the surgery we contrived to give Edal a general anaesthetic by pumping ether into a tea chest air-sealed with towels. She took a long time to lose consciousness, and all the time she screamed like a wounded hare, a sound so utterly piteous that I found my hands unsteady and a cold sweat coming out on my forehead. When at length she was unconscious the vet found it impossible to shift the molar. It resisted every normal means of extraction, and he was afraid of damaging the jaw or skull if he used greater force. Seeing her lying there inert on the operating table, draggled and with her

mouth full of blood, I did not believe in her recovery.

We got her back into the Land-Rover just before
she came round from the anaesthetic; through the
rear window I could see her, dazed and blood-
stained, walking in stumbling circles. I am baby
enough to have been very near to tears.

At the end of the two-hour journey I felt a spark
of hope; she was able to walk down the hill, and
though she was noticeably off balance I thought
this to be the after-effects of the anaesthetic.
She would not eat, but in the circumstances
that seemed natural enough. We managed to
get her into her own upstairs quarters; there she
appeared to go to sleep, and we left her for the
night.

In the morning the local vet came – I say local
for want of a better word, for he lives more than
fifty miles away by road and sea-ferry. I was totally unprepared for the rapid overnight worsen-
ing in Edal's condition, and I opened her door to
bring her downstairs. She was partly paralysed and
wholly mad. She fell rather than walked down the
stairs, and stumbled out into the garden, where she
toppled over on her side, kicking and twitching.
When she came out of this she raised herself un-
steadily and looked around her with mad eyes for
something to attack. Finally – for despite the
paralysis she seemed enormously strong – she man-

aged to get into the kitchen and scramble into a wooden armchair with a slot back. Here she was unapproachable, screaming and literally gnashing her teeth at the least sign of movement in the room.

The vet looked at her and said nothing; I took his silence for a death warrant. I knew that in a month's time, when my book was published, Edal would have been a famous animal. I telephoned to London, not because I had been asked to do so but because I felt it unfair to put all the responsibility upon this young man. I described the situation as well as I could, and the advice I received over the telephone was plain. Had I got a gun in the house? I had a pistol, and only one round; I searched for it before returning to the kitchen. It was only a question of ways and means now. But the young vet, with his slow, considered, Highland speech, said, 'It is not fair to consult a practitioner six hundred miles from the patient; he is not on the spot and he has no opportunity to form an opinion as he would like. A bullet will prove nothing, and also it would spoil the body for post-mortem. I think there is a very faint chance, and if you are willing to try I am. We shall have to give her very massive injections of antibiotics daily for five days, and if there is no improvement then she will go into a coma and die quietly.' I felt, and I expect looked, helpless. How were we going to get near enough to this unrecognizable creature to touch her, let alone inject her?

We had one small help – the slotted back to the chair on which she was sitting. While I distracted her attention from the front, Jimmy Watt managed somehow to slip a lead on to her harness through the gaps in the woodwork. Then, by using a shepherd's crook, I managed to lift the lead through until it was on the same side of the chair as she was. We slipped the loop of another lead down over this one so that she could be held from two different directions and in this way moved her slowly off the chair until we could take a turn of one lead round a kitchen table-leg. Then we drew the other lead tight too, and I took hold of her tail. Even when she was held from three points and could not turn her head it must have been like trying to inject a flying bird, but that vet did it. Then we put on rubber thigh boots and half-hoisted half-dangled her up the stairs and back into her own room.

For the following four days we repeated the same procedure, but always in her room, and each day the vet showed the same fantastic skill in injecting his moving target. We entered that room only in thigh boots, and always as we went about the daily routine of cleaning the floor and changing her water she would drag her paralysed hind-quarters after her in pathetic efforts to attack.

Then at last came a day when as I entered the room I seemed to see something different about her appearance. She was curled up in her bed in the corner, and she seemed to look at me questioningly, as if I had been away for a long time and she was not sure if it could be me. I came nearer, and she suddenly gave a little whimper of recognition as she had been used to when she was pleased to see me or Jimmy. With great hesitation I gave her the back of my bare hand to sniff, and the greeting noises redoubled. I knew then that however long her physical paralysis might remain she was mentally normal. I got down on the floor beside her and put my face down to her and stroked her, and she rubbed her whiskers over my cheeks and pushed her nose into my neck while all the time she whimpered her welcome and affection for someone who had been away for so long.

Physically, her recovery took a long time, but it progressed just as the vet had hoped; a returning power in her front limbs, then her hind limbs, and last of all the ability to move her tail. Very slowly, over a period of months, she regained the full use of all her muscles, began to play again, and to gallop and to swim and to dive. Now she is once again her old delightful self, and that awful week that began on Sunday, 7 August 1960, seems now like a nightmare that cannot really have happened. One day early in November I found her playing on the floor with a new toy that she had somewhere discovered; it was the single round of pistol ammunition with which I had been going to end her life.

About the Author

Gavin Maxwell was the youngest son of Lieut. Col. Aymer Maxwell and was born in 1914 at the House of Elrig, Wigtownshire, and educated at Stowe and Hertford College, Oxford. His grandfather was the celebrated archaeologist, politician and natural historian, Sir Herbert Maxwell of Monreith, K.I.

Before the war he was a freelance journalist and also went on an ornithological expedition to East Finnmark. During the war he served in the Scots Guards before being seconded to Special Forces, and was invalided out with the rank of Major in 1944. After the war he bought the Island of Soay in the Hebrides. He became a professional portrait painter in 1949, and contributed poetry and prose to well-known weeklies. In 1956 he published *God Protect Me from My Friends*, a biography of the 'bandit' Salvatore Giuliano (which won him 8 months' prison sentence in Italy), and in 1958 *A Reed Shaken by the Wind*, an account of travels in Southern Iraq (for which he won the Heinemann Award of the Royal Society of Literature). In 1960 appeared *Ring of Bright Water*, which became a top best-seller.

Gavin Maxwell died in 1969.

WATERSHIP DOWN
Richard Adams

One dim, moonlit night a small band of rabbits leave the comfort and safety of their warren, and set out on a long and dangerous journey. A dramatic and totally gripping bestseller.

GREYFRIARS BOBBY
Eleanor Atkinson

A touching, true story about the little Skye terrier who returned every night for fourteen years to the shepherd's grave in Greyfriars churchyard – so dearly had he loved his master.

THE SHEEP-PIG
Dick King-Smith

The wonderful story about the sheep-dog Fly who adopts Babe the piglet and trains him to be a sheep-dog!

LASSIE COME – HOME
Eric Knight

The classic heartwarming story of a dog and her devotion, who travels hundreds of miles so that she can meet a boy by the school-house gate and be faithful to her duty.

THE MOUSE AND HIS CHILD
Russell Hoban

The epic journey of the father mouse and his child from the toyshop to their eventual home.

A DOG CALLED NELSON
Bill Naughton

A real-life story about a one-eyed mongrel of remarkable character called Nelson. A lively, humorous and touching tale.

MRS FRISBY AND THE RATS OF NIMH
Robert C. O'Brien

A fabulous adventure about the mysterious, ultra-intelligent rats, their past and their secret connection with Mrs Frisby's late husband.

CHARLOTTE'S WEB
E. B. White

The tale of how a little girl called Fern, with the help of a friendly spider, manages to save her beloved pig Wilbur from the usual fate of nice fat little pigs.

TARKA THE OTTER
Henry Williamson

The classic tale of an otter's life and death in Devon is as true as a man's account of a wild animal can possibly be. This book was hailed as a masterpiece when first published and today Tarka is one of the best-loved creatures in world literature.